Henry William Bunbury

Annals of Horsemanship

containing accounts of accidental experiments, and experimental accidents -

communicated by various correspondents to Geoffrey Gambado

Henry William Bunbury

Annals of Horsemanship

containing accounts of accidental experiments, and experimental accidents - communicated by various correspondents to Geoffrey Gambado

ISBN/EAN: 9783337410032

Printed in Europe, USA, Canada, Australia, Japan

Cover: Foto ©Andreas Hilbeck / pixelio.de

More available books at **www.hansebooks.com**

A N N A L S

OF

H O R S E M A N·S H I P :

CONTAINING ACCOUNTS OF

ACCIDENTAL EXPERIMENTS,

AND

EXPERIMENTAL ACCIDENTS,

BOTH SUCCESSFUL AND UNSUCCESSFUL :

COMMUNICATED BY VARIOUS CORRESPONDENTS

TO

GEOFFREY GAMBADO, ESQ.

AUTHOR OF THE ACADEMY FOR GROWN HORSEMEN;

TOGETHER WITH

MOST INSTRUCTIVE REMARKS THEREON, AND ANSWERS THERETO,
BY THAT ACCOMPLISHED GENIUS.

AND NOW FIRST PUBLISHED,

BY THE EDITOR OF THE ACADEMY FOR *GROWN HORSEMEN.*

ILLUSTRATED WITH CUTS BY THE MOST EMINENT ARTISTS.

D U B L I N :

PRINTED FOR WILLIAM JONES, NO. 86, DAME-STREET.

1 7 9 2.

THE

E D I T O R

TO THE

R E A D E R.

THE Public is in high luck to obtain any thing more that comes from the pen of Geoffrey Gambado. A former publication has nearly immortalized him, and I truſt the preſent will do it completely. It is true this work is chiefly compoſed of Letters addreſt to him, but his remarks and replies are added to them; and had it not been for Geoffrey, ſuch letters had never made their appearance; perhaps never been written. What had been ſuch a loſs to the community! I will venture to affirm that few,

a   very

very few, have heard of such extraordinary
cases, such novel ideas, and such obvious and
salutary advice as are contained in the following pages. Were I to mention the odd
place in which I found the MSS. copy of
this work, it might create laughter.——

" A paſſion hateful to my purpoſes."

For having the ſafety of man's neck in my
eye at this preſent writing, I think it no
laughing matter; and ſhall therefore deem it
ſufficient to ſay, I have found it, and have
now the ſatisfaction of laying it before the
world.

A paltry publication has lately made its
appearance, on the ſame conſtruction as this.
It is a periodical thing, entitled The Annals
of Agriculture, and will, I dare ſay, be of
much uſe in the chandlers ſhops. This too,
like Geoffrey's edifying collection of letters,
treats on propagation, cultivation, preſerva-
tion, the good of the nation, &c. &c. But
when

when we once confider for a moment the different objects the authors claim our attention in behalf of—Should even a potatoe enter the lifts with a poncy, my blood rifes—my choler is excited.

Talk of propagation! Would the blockheads have us hefitate between a horfe chefnut, and a chefnut horfe! Common fenfe forbids it (particularly as it is to be the fafhionable colour in harnefs this time five years); and as for prefervation—Which fhould humanity firft extend her arm to fave? A cabbage or a cockney—A captain or a cauliflower? For thefe reafons I lament feeing, monthly, the names of feveral refpectable friends of mine, affixed to a work of fuch fubordinate confideration. Had they fpent as much time in riding upon turnips, as they have in writing upon them, they might ere now have belonged to the firft hunts in the country, and moft fafhionable clubs in town. But I fear the filk purfe and the fow s ear are but too applicable to moft of them.

In

In the ladies, however, Geoffrey will undoubtedly find warm advocates. Thofe love-
ly creatures, who delight fo much in the
propagation of their own beautiful fpecies,
will ever fupport the Animal Syftem in
preference to the Vegetable; nor wafte their
precious time and confideration on a carrot,
which may be fo much better employed in
furnifhing a cradle.

And whilft the frantic farmers that furnifh their ftuff for the Annals of Agriculture, fhall be puzzling their brains to preferve a ragged flock of fheep from the rot,
the fair fex fhall be more nobly employed
in the prefervation of beauty, and what is
more puzzling, though we daily fee it attempted—the prefervation of even The Hu-
man Face Divine, itfelf.

Emboldened by thefe confiderations, that
the Annals of Horfemanfhip will fpeedily
drive the Annals of Agriculture out of the
houfe of every man and woman of tafte
and

and feeling, I do not hefitate to forefee.
From his anfwers to fome of the following
letters it appears, that Mr. Gambado was
fomewhat irritable, as in a poftfcript, page
7, he rather fnubs his correfpondent for afk-
ing his advice. It fhould likewife feem that
he was at this time rather fhort of cafh, for
he appears to have given advice for a fee;
and once, if I recollect, treats of bad fhil-
lings. This, indeed, might a little four his
natural difpofition, which I have reafon to
believe, from his phyfiognomy, was placid and
amiable. I am told he feldom rode himfelf;
and the only time he went fix miles on
horfeback, he wore a pair of Diaculum drawers.
That fuch an author fhould be no rider may
appear marvellous at firft, but, on reflection,
we muft acknowledge that we daily find people fpeaking and writing on what they
know nothing at all about. Herein Geoffrey
exceeds all I ever heard of: for fuch a book
of knowledge as his Academy for Grown
Horfemen, never yet made an appearance in
the world.

The

The Editor, therefore, of The Academy for Grown Horfemen has now to congratulate the public on the difcovery of another work from the pen of the much-admired Geoffrey Gambado; a work that contains fome of the moft ufeful and extraordinary experiments, perhaps, ever made in Horfemanfhip: feveral curious cuftoms and opinions of ingenious gentlemen, little known to the world, and fome collected from very choice, but remote publications; together with (what will be no doubt efteemed invaluable) Geoffrey's moft ingenious fuggeftions, and prefcriptions towards the removal of every difficulty and danger incidental to that moft noble art: his anfwers to fome queries put to him, and his criticifms on others that were un-anfwerable.

By the putting forth of this work the public muft be let into much ufeful knowledge. The many practical attempts and atchievements herein recorded prove, beyond a doubt, that fuch things have been; and having been, that in all probability fuch things are. And even thofe experiments that have not been attended,

tended, hitherto, with perfect fuccefs, may yet, like balloons, turn out to the moft valuable account, when taken into hand by more fkilful philofophers. The Editor here begs leave to remark, that the Diaculum Drawers abovementioned, are the only fabrics of the kind he ever heard of, and verily believes they are hitherto non-defcript. He has fome reafon to think they are yet extant (and fhould they be, they are worthy the fearch of the Dilettanti) ; for a fort of flannel breeches, apparently prepared in the fame manner, but much damaged by time, &c. were laft week offered to the Leverian Mufeum, but are faid, for delicate reafons, to have been rejected by the proprietor as unfit for exhibition. What falfe delicacy ! when the man pefters us every day with a non-defcript in the papers ; fome old ftinking fifh, that never could be of fervice to man, woman, or beaft ! whereas the drawers, like the North-weft paffage, if they could be once difcovered, might prove hereafter of the greateft fundamental confequence to mankind at large, the Venetians only excepted.

THE EDITOR.

DIRECTIONS TO THE BINDER.

1. Apotheofis of Geoffrey Gambado - To front the Title.

2. Gambado feeing the World - - - Page xiv

3. The Puzzle - - - - - - 2

4. ———— for a Dog, Horfe, or Chriftian - - 3

5. How to make the moft of him - - - 20

6. ———— the leaft of him - - - - 23

7. How to do things by Halves - - - - 29

8. Tricks upon Travellers - - - - 32

9. Love and Wind - - - - - - 36

10. Me, my Wife and Daughter - - - - 45

11. How to make the Mare to go - - - - 64

12. How to prevent a Horfe flipping his Girths - - 72

13. How to ride without a Bridle - - - - 74

14. The Daifey Cutter - - - - - 80

15. The Tumblers, or its Affinities - - - 82

16. A Horfe with a Nofe - - - - - ib.

17. How to travel upon two Legs - - - - 94

ADVERTISEMENT.

I T clearly appears from the preface to the following Work, that it was compiled prior to Mr. Gambado's appointment of Maſter of the Horſe to the Doge of Venice; for it ſeems he had never at that time been above ſix miles from home.

To moſt of the Plates the Editor has thought fit to ſubjoin Latin mottos, as an elucidation of them to ſuch of his Readers as do not underſtand Engliſh; and ſuch he may perhaps meet with.

b

GEOFFREY GAMBADO

TO THE READER.

I FLATTER myfelf the following com-
pilation will not prove unwelcome to the
Public; it blends information with amufement, and confirms how general is the thirft
for knowledge in the prefent times, which
is not to be idly checked by the lofs of a
limb or a life. The adventurers of this
age are divided into two clafles—*per mare,
per terras*—of which latter defcription are
my correfpondents. Thofe of the former,
fancy they difcover much, by being at fea
for months together without fight of land
—by the wanting wine and water, and get-

ting

ting neither—but at length efpying fomething like an ifland unknown ; it is perhaps
more like an owzle than any one laid down
in the charts.   They do actually difcover,
however, that the natives will not let them go
afhore, and that they muft return as wife as
they came.   They difcover that they have
little left to eat, and lefs to drink ; that they
muft live by fucking each others fhirts for half
a year, arrive miraculoufly at home, and write
a book about it.

My Correfpondents are of a different ftamp ;
they difcover that there is much left unfound
out at home ; and feem to be meritorioufly
employed in confequence.   Going abroad, with
them, I take to be only going out of the
houfe and feeing the world, a laudable ride
of a dozen miles.   This opinion of feeing the
world tempts me to digrefs a little.   My apo-
thecary, a man of knowledge and judgment,
but who, no more than myfelf, had ever been
above fix miles from home, being obliged
to vifit a patient at the diftance of twenty,
actually returned in amazement, and affured
                                                    me,

Mr. Gainsboro' seeing the World in a Six Mile Tour so famed in History

LAKES, FORESTS, CITIES, PLAINS EXTENDED WIDE,

THE POMP OF KINGS, THE SHEPHERDS HUMBLER PRIDE.

me, he could not have thought the world was fo big. Thefe were his very words—and was not it mighty natural?

To fhew how much of the natural he had in him, I cannot refrain from adding, that, having paft a turnpike or two, for the firft time, in this excurfion, he was in raptures at the piety of the people thereabouts; for he told me, that they had the Belief and the Ten Commandments painted upon blue boards at every gate—though he paft through and could not read them, having left his fpectacles at home.

Pardon, gentle Reader, this digreffion, which has informed you of an anecdote rather extraordinary. If you do not believe it, and fhould find out the fubject, who was him-felf the narrator; don't venture to tell him fo—He is a paffionate man, rather inclined to let blood, and may perhaps, if you commit yourfelf to him, put you to death.

To return to bufinefs—The letters I have received have required a clever arrangement; and

and I thought it better to add my anfwers, or
remarks, immediately to each, than to hud-
dle the letters into one part, and the anfwers
into a fecond.   Cuts were alfo thought neceffary towards the clearing up of fome of the
moft blind defcriptions of awkward fituations
and queer accidents which, I confefs, are, here
and there, but lamely made out by the writers.
I wifh my delineator may have fucceeded in
thofe I fet him to.   Several I have received,
inclofed in letters from the fufferers, or experimental philofophers themfelves, many of
which are frightfully defcriptive.

I requeft my Readers will be more attentive
to what is contained in the following pages, than
they were to my Hiftory of Cruppers, this
being of a much more ferious tendency—and a
publication that for its falutary or wholfome
advice ought to be printed for brafs*.   Some
of the letters, indeed, border on frivolity, and
fome even on folly; but as they may divert,
though

---

* Left the Printer fhould forget his *erratum*, I muft fuggeft,
that Mr. G. could never mean FOR but IN brafs.

Mr. G. mentions his Hiftory of Cruppers—a work new to my ears
—but I fhall be diligent in my fearch after it.

though they will not inftruct, I fhall not omit
them ; for bread, though taftelefs, makes a fa-
vory difh go down the better.   And that this
book may go down, I mean with the Town,
now, and to Pofterity by and by, when it has
ferved its time and my turn here (for I expect
fome fame from it), is the very earneft wifh of,
courteous Reader, your very faithful humble
Servant,

G. GAMBADO.

LETTER THE FIRST.

MR. GAMBADO!

I RETURN you my moſt hearty thanks for the very ſalutary advice you ſent me laſt month, from which I have derived much improvement, and ſhould have acknowledged ſooner, had I made ſufficient trial of the fine machine you recommended in ſuch warm terms. My Hobby, as I told you before, is an admirable animal, and finely calculated for a penſive man, like myſelf, to take the air upon. It was a pity he was ſo prone to tumble, and that too, in ſtony roads the moſt; for he was otherwiſe bordering on perfection. So I ſent for a carpenter, on the receipt of your recipe, and had a large Puzzle of Oak made for him, after

B   the

the pattern of thofe worn by the Squire's Pointers; and I have found it anfwer prodigioufly.

I have had nothing like a bad fall lately, except one day in cantering over a ploughed field, where, upon a blunder, the machine entered the ground with fuch force as to introduce a portion of the Hobby's head along with it. We came clean over, and for fome time I thought my Hobby's neck was broke. I did not mind it myfelf, but I fhall take care in future always to gallop on the hard road, and then fuch another cataftrophe cannot enfue.

I am, Sir,

Your moft obfequious humble Servant,

CALEB CASSOCK.

Eye, Suffolk.

P. S. I forgot to tell you my Parifhioners ftare at me a good deal. The Machine has an odd appearance, I own; but not altogether unpicturefque. I got the Drawingmafter of Mr. Birch's fchool to fend you a fketch of me.

It

Dr CASSOCK F.RS. T.P.Q. *Inventor of the noble Puzzle for tumble-down* HORSES.

TE, VENIENTE DIE, TE DECEDENTE CANEBAM

The Puzzle for the Horse

The Puzzle for Turk, Frenchman or Christian?

It is efteemed a likenefs. That of the Hobby is rather flattering.

I have fent you alfo a fketch of my Puzzle for Dog and Horfe, and a fcheme for puzzling a Chriftian.

C. C

MY REMARKS.

I am happy to find the Puzzle has anfwered fo well; and I doubt not, now it has been tried and approved by fuch a right-headed, Reverend Gentleman, one who is alfo fo good a horfeman, and underftands all the matter fo well, that, by producing his name, I fhall be able to get a patent for it, which cannot but prove very lucrative; for who has the horfe that he will fwear will never tumble down?

This I believe would be a queftion that would pofe (upon oath) every man on horfeback in Hyde Park on a Sunday.

Though Dr. Shaw himfelf, who is a great traveller indeed, has the modefty to affure us, that the Barbary horfes never lie down; yet even he has not the effrontery to fay that they never tumble down!

I received the fketches of the Puzzles of Dogs and Horfes; and hold it fit an etching fhould be made of them, for the information of thofe who never faw fuch machines.

The fcheme for puzzling Chriftians, I fuppofe, dropt out of the letter, for I never got it. There are, however, fo

B 2   many

many fchemes of that fort already about town, that it is no
lofs, I dare fay.

G. G.

My Correfpondent, I believe, did not diflike fitting for
his picture—there appears fuch an amiable fmirk in his countenance, and he fays too it is efteemed a likenefs.

Note to Letter the Firft.

Although this Puzzle for a Chriftian, as he calls it, was dropt,
I can conceive its being of ufe, if put upon one of thofe long
ftory-tellers who catch hold of your button, and thruft their
nofe and mouth in your face, when perhaps it is highly neceffary to keep them at arms length. In the adjoining Plate,
therefore, are delineated not only the Canini and Equeftrian,
but alfo the Chriftian Puzzle.

LETTER

LETTER THE SECOND.

SIR,

YOUR fame having reached us here, I fet down with pleafure to write to a man who I am certain will have an equal pleafure in fatisfying the doubts that now occupy my mind. I would proceed and ftate every difficulty I find in the treatment and guidance of a horfe, to which animal I confefs I am rather an alien, although I have happily attained (yefterday it was) my thirty-fifth year. I was bred to a bufinefs that debarred me from an amufement for which I feem formed by nature, being, Sir, very fhort in the fork, and what our wits call duck legged, and all my weight lying atop: and it was not till I emerged, as I may fay, from the counting houfe, that I could make

a trial

a trial of my abilities as a horfeman. I really
think I am going on well, that I am in a
ftate of daily amendment and progreffive
improvement. The queftions I have to put
to you Sir are fo fhort and fimple that I will
not divert your attention from them a bit
longer, but put them down as they arife—
they require nothing but an anfwer.

QUERIES.

1. What part of my horfe muft I lay hold of to help
me up, for his mane is cut off?

2. If he will turn to the left when I want to go to the
right, how can I help it?

3. If he flips his girths, and the crupper is of no ufe,
what will fupply its place?

4. Should he tumble down by day-light, whether you
think he would in the dark?

5. What a breaft-plate is? We have heard of it here,
but our Saddler does not know how to make one. The
Adjutant of the Militia fays it is a fort of armour, to prevent the horfe hurting himfelf by running againft a waggon
or a wall. But I fay it can't be; becaufe the horfe's head
fhould be armed, as that would hit the wall firft, and prevent his breaft receiving any damage. Pray folve this by return

turn of poſt, as many betts are depending on it at our next Club.

6. How can I keep a horſe cheap?

7. What is my beſt way to ſell a bad horſe, if I don't like him?

Theſe are a few of the trifling queſtions I ſhall beg leave to trouble you with from time to time: and as it will be extremely eaſy, and, I dare ſay, agreeable to you, to anſwer them, I ſhall make no apology but with my aſſurance that I am, Sir,

Your devoted and very humble Servant,

SAMUEL FILLAGREE.

G. Gambado, Eſq.

_____

This fellow, with his aſſurance, appeared to be ſuch a puppy, I could not anſwer him for ſome months; indeed his queries rather poſed me; but his fees came in faſt, and I was fain to ſolve them as well as I could.

The firſt I left to his better judgment, only ſuggeſting that the ear of the horſe and the pommel of the ſaddle were all that

that offered themselves in lieu of a mane, if his horse had none.

The second I could not affist him in.

The folly of the third raised my choler, and involving with it the fifth, I had not patience to enter on either of them; fo I fear the betts at the Club are not yet decided.

The fourth and fixth were extremely eafy to be anfwered; I never met with two queries more fo. But the feventh, fkilful as I am, I confefs I could not reply to, to my Correfpondent's fatisfaction: and I fhall be much bound to any of my Readers, who will tell me, how the bufinefs therein ftated is to be brought about; being ever open to conviction, and not yet too old to learn.

G. G.

LETTER

LETTER THE THIRD.

From a Half-way Houſe between Cambridge and Newmarket.

MARCH 26, 1789.

SIR,

HAVING long been earneſtly engaged in the ſtudy of mathematical ſcience, and being fond of riding, two purſuits uſually thought incompatible, I have been enabled, by means of this ſingular union, to ſtrike out ſome important diſcoveries in both branches. The mathematical improvements in riding will, I hope, deſerve a place in the Annals of Horſemanſhip: my equeſtrian diſcoveries in mathematics you muſt permit me to reſerve for the Ladies Diary.

My love for equeſtrian agitation is, I be-lieve, more general than that of any other perſon; for whatever ſatisfaction may be

C   uſually

uſually experienced by riders while they con-
tinue on the backs of their horſes, I have
never yet met with or been informed of one,
who received any ſenſible delight from the
circumſtance of being violently projected from
the ſaddle. But here, Sir, from my paſſionate
fondneſs for the mathematics, I enjoy a ma-
nifeſt advantage. From the concuſſions, re-
percuſſions, and every other kind of compound motion which can be generated con-
ſiſtently with the due ſupport of the centre
of gravity, I enjoy, I will venture to ſay, at
leaſt as much ſatisfaction as any other rider :
and at the time of being thrown off, or, in
more proper language, projected from the
horſe, I experience a peculiar delight in re-
collecting that, by the univerſal laws of pro-
jectiles, I muſt, in my flight through the
air, deſcribe that beautiful conic ſection, a
parabola.

After ſome accidents of this nature, I have
been fortunate enough, notwithſtanding the
violent re-action of the ground in conſequence
of the ſtrong action of my ſkull againſt it, to
preſerve

preſerve my ſenſe ſufficiently to be able to
aſcertain the curve ſo generated by my body
to deſcribe it on paper, and demonſtrate its
peculiar properties : and am not without
hope, if I can meet with horſes not too
ſure-footed, by frequent experiments, to determine what kind of parabola it is ſafeſt to
deſcribe ; which problem will, I apprehend,
be found very ſerviceable in practice, at the
City Hunt in Eaſter week, and during the cele-
bration of Epſom races.

Not long ago, by a particular convulſion
of the animal from which I was ſo fortunate as to fall, I was very irregularly thrown
to the earth, but had the ſatisfaction afterwards to diſcover that the curve deſcribed in
my fall was a ſegment of a very eccentric
ellipſe, of which the ſaddle was one focus ;
and that it was nearly, if not exactly, the
ſame with the path of the comet now ex-
pected to return.   And once, by a ſuccuſſation,
ſtill more anomalous, I was happy enough to
deſcribe a new curve, which I found to poſ-
ſeſs ſome very amazing properties ; and I

hope

hope effectually to immortalize my own name, by calling it *Angle's firſt Hippopiptic* * *curve.*

The firſt equeſtrian problem that I ever ſet myſelf to diſcover was this; " When by pulling the reins you prevent a horſe from falling, where is the fulcrum or prop ?—and how is the horſe's centre of gravity prevented from being thrown beyond the baſe of his legs ?" I will not trouble you now with the particulars of this difficult inveſtigation; but ſhall only ſay, that it turned out greatly to the honour of demipique ſaddles; which, accordingly, in the Mathematical Elements of Riding, that I mean hereafter to publiſh, I ſhall recommend very ſtrongly in a Corollary.

A learned

---

* *Hippopiptic* expreſſes the mode of the curve's generation in falling from a horſe :—from *Hippos*, a horſe, and *pipto*, to fall. I call it *firſt*, becauſe I hope by the ſame means to diſcover more hereafter.

A learned Student in Mathematics has long publifhed his ability and defire to conftruct breeches upon geometrical principles *.

Mr. Nunn is certainly ingenious, and his breeches, a few falient angles excepted, admirable; but the artift who fhould make bridles, faddles, and other equeftrian paraphernalia, by the rules of pure mathematics, would render a much more praife-worthy fervice to the public. For if the flimfy leather breeches require geometrical cutting, how much more neceffary muft it be to the tough hide which forms the bridle? and to what purpofe will the geometry in the breeches operate, if the faddle, by which they are to be

---

* Mr. Nunn's advertifement is as follows:

"BREECHES-MAKING IMPROVED BY GEOMETRY."

"Thomas Nunn, Breeches-maker, No. 29, Wigmore-ftreet, Cavendifh-fquare, has invented a fyftem on a mathematical principle, by which difficulties are folved, and errors corrected: its ufefulnefs for eafe and neatnefs in fitting, is incomparable, and is the only perfect rule for that work ever difcovered. Several hundreds (noblemen, gentlemen, and others) who have had proof of its utility, allow it to excel all they ever made trial of."

be fupported, and whofe fuperficies they are to touch in as many points as poffible, be formed ungeometrically? But I forbear to expatiate on a matter as plain as an axiom of Euclid; trufting, that whoever can perceive the utility of geometrical breeches, will readily agree, *à fortiori*, to the abfolute neceffity of geometrical faddles and bridles.

Purfuing my principles, I have demonftrated what is the right line to be drawn by the mathematical rider in every difficult fituation. In afcending a horfe's back, at what angle to extend the moveable leg, while the fixed one is refted in the ftirrup: in leaping, how to regulate the ofcillation, or balancing of the body, by attending carefully to that fundamental point which is your centre of motion: in ftarting, how to difpofe of the fuperfluous momentum, and thereby to preferve in full force the attraction of cohefion between rump and faddle: in rearing, at what angle, formed by the horfe's back with the plane of the horizon, it is moft advifable to flide down over his tail; which,

which, I maintain, is the only expedient
that can be practised with a mathematical
certainty of being safe: these, and many
other important secrets, I am ready, at any
time when called upon, to communicate.
One I cannot even now withhold, which is
this: that there is no good or truly geometrical riding, unless the legs be extended
perfectly in straight lines, so as to form tan-
gents to the cylindrical surface of the horse's
body: in a word, to resemble, as much as
possible, a pair of compasses set astride upon
a telescope; which I conceive to be the
perfect model of mathematical riding.

But besides this application of pure geometry, it has often struck me, that too little
use is made, in riding, of the principles of
mixed mathematics. Consider, Mr. Gambado, the six mechanical powers! the *lever*,
the *wheel and axle*, the *pulley*, the *inclined
plane*, the *wedge*, and the *screw*; and reflect
with what advantage all these may be applied to the uses of Horsemanship. By means
of a *lever*, having an elevated fulcrum raised

on

on the pommel of the faddle, an entire ftop might be put to the practice of falling; except where the practitioner fhould voluntarily take a tumble, for the exprefs purpofe of ftudying the Parabola, or Hippopiptic Curve. The *wheel and axle* is already applied in the ufe of horfes, though not in any branch of Horfemanfhip, except the driving of poft-chaifes; it is alfo found fo efficacious in preventing falls, that where a horfe has been ufed to that affiftance, it is not reckoned fafe to ride him without it. The application of the *wedge* might, undoubtedly, very materially improve the art of figging. The *fcrew* might, with advantage, be applied to the direction of the horfe's head with more exactnefs, and confequently enable the rider to guide his courfe with mathematical accuracy. The *inclined plane* might happily be introduced to facilitate the backward flide of the rider at the time of rearing, as above mentioned. And a fyftem of *pullies*, in the nature of Mr. Smeaton's, by giving the rider a force equal to the action of many thoufand pounds weight, might

for

for ever put an end to the dangerous vice of running away.

By the ufe of the principles of aftronomy, I have invented a mode of taking the exact altitude of any horfe, at two obfervations; and am at prefent at work on a Hippodromometer*, to afcertain the velocity of his courfe in the very act of riding.

But while I boaft, and, I truft, with reafon, of thefe difcoveries, I muft candidly confefs that a rigorous attention to theory has fometimes betrayed me into practical errors. When my horfe has been pulling earneftly one way, my own intention being at the fame time to go another, I have pulled ftrongly at right angles to the line of his courfe; expecting, from the laws of compound motion, that we fhould then proceed, neither in the line of his effort nor of my pull, but in an intermediate one, which would be the diagonal of the parallelogram, of which our forces were as the fides; but have always found that

D   this

---

* From *Hippos* a horfe, *dromos* a courfe, and *metrein* to meafure.

this method produced a rotatory inftead of a rectilinear motion. When a horfe has run away, I have, to avoid the wafte of force in my own arms, calculated the neceffary diminution of it in his legs; but, unfortunately, eftimating it as the fquares of the diftances multiplied into the times, I was frequently dafhed againft walls, pitched over gates, and plunged into ponds, before I difcovered that it is not as the fquares of the times, but merely as the times. I mention thefe circumftances by way of caution to other theorifts; not being at all difcouraged myfelf by fuch trifling failures, and hoping, by your affiftance, to convince the world that no man can ever become a perfect rider, unlefs he has firft made mathematics his hobby-horfe. You will pardon this innocent play of words on a fubject fo ferious, and believe me to be, Sir, with great efteem,

Yours, &c.

HABAKKUK ANGLE.

LETTER

LETTER THE FOURTH.

To Mr. G. GAMBADO.

SIR,

I WANT your advice, and hope you will give it me, concerning a horfe I have lately bought, and which does not carry me at all in the fame way he did the man I bought him of. Being recommended to a Dealer in Moorfields (who I rather think is no honefter than he ought to be), I went to him, and defired to look into his ftable, and fo he took me in; with a long whip in his hand, which he faid was to wake the horfes that might perhaps be afleep, as they were but juft arrived from a long journey, coming frefh

D 2   from

from the breeder in the North. There were
fome fine looking geldings, I thought, and I
pitched upon one that I thought would fuit
me ; and fo he was faddled, and I defired the
Dealer to mount him, and he did, and a very
fine figure the gelding cut ; and fo the people
in the ftreet faid ; and a decent man, in a
fcratch wig, faid, the man that rode him knew
how to make the moft of him ; and fo I
bought him.   But he goes in a different
manner with me, for inftead of his capering
like a Trooper, he hangs down his head
and tail, and neither whip nor fpur can get
him out of a fnail's gallop.   And I want to
know whether by law I muft keep him,
as he is not certainly the horfe I took him
for ; and therefore I ought to have my money
again.

The Limner in our lane was with me
when I bought him, and has taken a picture
of him as he was with the Dealer on his
back, and another as he now goes with me
upon his back ; by which you will fee the
dif-

How to make the most of a Horse

difference, and judge better how to advise me upon it.

> I am, Sir, your humble Servant,
> TOBIAS HIGGINS.

Lavender Row, Shoreditch.

Please to direct to Mr. *T. H.* Back-maker; or it may go to my Namesake, the Turn-cock.

Reply

Reply to Letter the Fourth.

SIR,

UPON a ſtrict examination of the two pictures by the Limner in your lane, I am clear you are in poſſeſſion of the identical horſe you intended to purchaſe, although he does not exhibit quite ſo much agility under you, or make ſo tearing a figure as when mounted by Mr. ——— who I am well acquainted with, and who, you may depend upon, is as honeſt a man as any that deals in horſe fleſh. You could have no right to return the horſe if he went no better than one with his legs tied. You ſtand in the predicament of Lord P———, who gave twenty guineas for Punch, and when he found he could not make him ſpeak, proſecuted the Puppet-ſhew-man; but my Lord Chief Juſtice ad-

adjudged the man to keep his money, and my Lord, his Punch, although he could not get a word out of him.

My opinion is, Sir, as you aſk it : that the decent man in the ſcratch wig made a very ſen-ſible remark, when he obſerved, that my friend Mr.———— knew how to make the moſt of a horſe, and I am ſatisfied that you, Sir, know with equal facility, how to make the leaſt of one.

I am, Sir, your humble Servant,

G. GAMBADO.

P. S. I am ſorry to add, my Maid tells me, that two ſhillings out of your five were very bad ones.

LETTER

LETTER THE FIFTH.

To G. GAMBADO, *Efq.*

SIR,

AS I confider you, both from your fituation and eminence in the fcience of Horfemanfhip, as the fuperior and patron of all
Riding Mafters, permit me an humble member of that honourable profeffion, to requeft
your countenance in my endeavours to diffufe
the noble and ufeful accomplifhment over the
whole kingdom.

It is well known that many of his Majefty's
faithful fubjects, whofe occupations oblige
them daily to figure as Equeftrians; fo far
from having been inftructed in the art of
Riding

Riding, are totally ignorant that any fuch art, or rather fcience, exifts. For the benefit of thefe, I propofe publifhing a Treatife on Horfemanfhip, confined to the lower claffes of life.

The firft part I fhall dedicate to the inftruction of that very numerous and brilliant fraternity, called London Riders, or Bagfters; who cut, or rather (as my Lord Chefterfield will have it) make fo fmart a figure in a country town; for thefe gentlemen, I propofe to point out and demonftrate, from irrefragable principles, the handfomeft manner of riding behind their bags, with the genteeleft method of rolling, ftrapping, and carrying their great coats. In a fhort digreffion, and a few marginal notes, I intend to drop fome hints, inftructing butchers in the fmarteft fafhion of carrying a tray, whether loaded or empty.

I fhall likewife rifque a few thoughts refpecting the theory and practice of the art of riding before a lady on a double horfe, vul-

E   garly

garly termed *à la gormagon*, with some neceffary inftructions thereon; a due attention
to which matters has more than once tranf-
planted a coachman from his box, or a
footman from behind the coach, and placed
him in the carriage by the fide of his Mif-
trefs.

I propofe alfo to devote part of my labours
to the fervice of the fair fex, in compofing
a fet of eafy rules for riding gracefully
between a pair of panniers, and fup-
porting a butter bafket in the moft elegant
ftile; a thorough poffeffion of thefe attrac-
tions may draw the attention of the fox-
hunting Squires, and poffibly raife the Lady
poffeffing them, to the dignity of Spoufe to his
Worfhip the Juftice.

That nothing may be wanting, I propofe to
appropriate a few pages to the art of fitting
politely in carriages, with the moft becom-
ing attitudes adopted to each vehicle.
Among others, the politeft manner of airing,
en famille, in a gig, accompanied with a huf-
band

band and three children; and, as there is no
fituation wherein art cannot be advantage-
oufly employed, I fhall give a few precepts
for the moft advantageous difplay of the perfon on a hay, pea, or duft cart. For the
ufe of both fexes, I had alfo digefted a few
hints and directions, pointing out the moft
folemn and affecting manner of riding in
a cart up Holborn Hill, from New-
gate to Tyburn; but the late adoption of
the New Drop has made them, in a great
meafure, ufelefs in London; they may however be ferviceable to perfons under fimilar
circumftances in country towns. As foon as
I have put my work together, I fhall beg
your opinion of it; being, Sir,

   Your humble Admirer,

    and moft obedient Servant,

      JAMES LA CROUPE.

The above Work, if well executed, promifes
to make a very pretty Supplement to mine.

      G. GAMBADO.

  E 2   LETTER

LETTER THE SIXTH.

SIR,

BEING informed that you are now at home, and defirous of giving every information in your power to thofe who may ftand in need of it, refpecting their Horfes, I beg leave to fubmit my cafe to you; which, confidering how fond I am of the chace, you muft admit to be a lamentable one. Relying however, Sir, as I do, on your Philanthropy (I fhould more properly fay Philippigy), and that zeal in the caufe which has fo long characterifed you, I make no doubt but the fmall difficulties I now labour under will be foon furmounted.

You

How to do things by...
STANT CÆTERA TIGNO.

You muſt know, Sir, I am very fond of
hunting, and live in as fine a ſcenting country
as any in the kingdom. The ſoil is pretty
ſtiff, the leaps large and frequent, and a
great deal of timber to get over. Now,
Sir, my brown horſe is a very capital hunter; and though he is ſlow, and I cannot
abſolutely ride over the hounds (indeed the
country is ſo encloſed, that I do not ſee ſo
much of them as I could wiſh), yet, in the
end, he generally brings me in before the
huntſman goes home with the dogs; ſo,
thus far, I have no reaſon to complain.
Now, Sir, my brown horſe is a noble leaper,
and never gave me a fall in his life in that
way; but he has got an awkward trick
(though he clears every thing with his fore
legs in a capital ſtile), of leaving the other
two on the wrong ſide of the fence; and
if the gate or ſtile happens to be in a ſound
ſtate, it is a work of time and trouble to get
his hind legs over. He clears a ditch finely
indeed, with two feet, but the others ſo
conſtantly fall in, that it gives me a ſtrange
pain

pain in my back, very like what is called a Lumbago; and unlefs you kindly ftand my friend, and inftruct me how I am to bring thefe hind legs after me, I fear I fhall never get rid of it. If you pleafe, Sir, you may ride him a hunting yourfelf any day you will pleafe to appoint, and you fhall be heartily welcome. You will then be better enabled to give me your advice; you can't have a proper conception of the jerks he will give you, without trying him.

I am, Sir, with due refpect,
Your very humble Servant,
NIC. NUTMEG, Clerk.

Hinderclay, near Botefdale,
Suffolk.

P. S. I hope what I have enclofed is gentcel.

Mr. Geoffrey Gambado.

The

The A N S W E R.

REVEREND SIR,

YOUR brown horfe being ſo good a hunter, and, as you obſerve, having ſo fine a
notion of leaping, I ſhould be happy if I
could be of any ſervice in aſſiſting you to
make his two hind legs follow the others;
but, as you obſerve, they ſeem ſo very
perverſe and obſtinate, that I cheriſh but ſmall
hopes of prevailing upon them.

I have look'd, and found many ſuch caſes,
but no cure. However, in examining my papers, I have found out ſomething that may
prove of ſervice to you, in your very lamentable
caſe.

An

An Hoſtler or (Oſteler, for ſo I believe it
is uſually written, though I find in the moſt
learned Dictionary in our language, which
explains ſome thouſands of words more than
Johnſon, that it is vulgarly and improperly
written Oſtteler, for Otſteler, query Oat-
ſtealer, and this, it muſt be allow'd, appears
to be the true word), an Otſteler then has
informèd me, that it is a common trick
play'd upon Bagſters, or London Riders,
when they are not generous to the ſervants
in the Inn, for a wicked boy or two to
watch one of them, as he turns out of the
gateway, and to pop a buſh or ſtick under
his horſe's tail, which he inſtantly brings
down upon the ſtick, and holds it faſt, kicking at the ſame time at ſuch a rate as to
diſlodge the Bagman that beſtrides him.
(The annexed Plate will ſhew how the ſtick
ſhould be placed).   Here, Sir, is a horſe
that lifts up his hind legs without mov-
ing his fore ones; and juſt the reverſe, as
I may ſay, of yours; and, perhaps, the hint
may be acceptable.   Suppoſe, then, when
your horſe has flown over a gate or a ſtile
in

Tricks upon Travellers.

in his old way, with his fore legs only, you were to difmount, and clap your whip, or ftick, properly under his tail, and then mount again ; the putting him in a little motion will fet him on his kicking principles in a hurry, and it's ten to one but, by this means, you get his hind legs to follow the others. You will be able, perhaps, to extricate your ftick from its place of confinement, when you are up and over (if you an't down) ; but fhould you not, it is but fixpence gone. I fend you this as a mere furmife ; perhaps it may anfwer, perhaps not.

I thank you for your offer, which is a very kind one, but I beg to be excufed accepting it ; all my ambition being to add to the theory, with as little practice as poffible.

I am, Rev. Sir, your moft humble Servant,

G. GAMBADO.

Rev. Nic. Nutmeg, Hinderclay, Suffolk.

N. B. What you enclofed was perfectly genteel, and agreeable too.

F   *Note.*

N O T E.

Mr. Gambado fhews more good writing, at leaft more knowledge of what good writing fhould be, in the beginning of the above Anfwer, than in any of his Letters. The judicious Reader will obferve that the Anfwer at firft is an echo of the Letter it replies to. This is approaching to excellence; it is bordering on the abilities of a Statefman; for fo the Minifter's addrefs re-echoes the fpeech from the Throne. Geoffrey's parts appear furely calculated for more places than one; and I do not fcruple to think it poffible, that, with a proper education, he might have been on the Treafury Bench; and a very pretty Statefman, I dare fay, he would have made.

N O T E.

The Dictionary above alluded to, is a very deep work : inftead of its containing more words by thoufands only than are in Johnfon —Johnfon does not give us ten words that are in it—nor does it contain much above ten words that are in Johnfon. No family fhould be without it, efpecially fuch as have plenty of young Mafters and Miffes in them; for it will at once fatisfy any little doubts in their unfledg'd underftandings, and let them into all the natural, but vulgar tricks and expreffions that they ought to avoid. This admirable Dictionary is entitled a Claffical Dictionary of the Vulgar Tongue.

N O T E.

If Lord Aboyne fhould lofe his Creft, which I don't fee how he can well do, I would advife him to adopt this print of Mr. Nutmeg's hunter, to which his Lordfhip's motto is finely applicable.

" *Stant cetera ligno.*"

LETTER

LETTER THE SEVENTH.

To G. GAMBADO, *Efq*.

SIR,

HEARING much of your knowledge in horfes, I beg leave to afk your advice in a bufinefs wherein my delicacy as a Gentleman is deeply concern'd, and flatter myfelf that you will fenfibly feel for my fituation, my future fortune in life in a great meafure depending on your decifion. I have the happinefs to be well received by a young Lady of fortune in this town, who rides out every morning, and has had the goodnefs to permit me to join her for fome days paft. I flatter myfelf I am belov'd; but,

F 2   ·Sir,

Sir, the horfe I ride is my Father's, and he will not allow me to part with him: and this horfe, Sir, has an infirmity of fuch an extreme indelicate nature, that our interviews are broke off every five minutes, and my dear Mifs S ——— will perhaps ride away with fome other Gownfman who is more decently mounted.

I really, Sir, dare not mention, in plain terms, the fhocking failing of my horfe; but, perhaps, if you look into Bailey's Dictionary, you may find it out under the article of Wind. Be pleas'd, Sir, to fend me a recipe for this horrid infirmity, or I may lofe my dear girl for ever, I have tried feveral experiments, but all in vain; and unlefs you ftand my friend, I fhall go diftracted.

Infandum Regina jubes renovare dolorem.

I am, my dear Sir,

In a great fufs, Your's moft truly,

GEORGE GILLYFLOWER.

St. John's Coll. Cambridge.

P. S.

Love and Wind.

JUVENUM PULCHERIMUS ALTER, ALTERA QUAS ORIENS HABET PRÆLATA PUELLIS

P. S. Regina is not her name, don't imagine that. May I be allow'd to fay, I am very anxious for an immediate anfwer, as fhe rides out again on Friday next.

Memorandum.

In confequence of the above, I fent the cafe to my Farrier, who forwarded directly fome powders to Mr. Gillyflower with the following Note. The efficacy being fo certain, the trifling indelicacy of the prefcription muft be excufed.

Honoured Sir,

By advice from Mr. Gambado of your horfe's complaint, I have fent you a powder fo ftrong, that if adminifter'd night and morning in his corn, will be bold to fay no horfe in England fhall ever fart again after
Thurfday

Thurfday next.   Shall be very thankful for
your Honour's cuftom in the fame way in
future, and your Lady's too, if agreeable; being, Honoured Sir,

Your Servant to command,

Jo. Wood.

At my Houfe at Chefhunt every day.   Horfes fhod agreeable to nature and according to art.

G. *Gillyflower*, *Efq. St. John's Coll. Cambridge.*

Additional Memorandum.

I thought it neceffary to employ my
Draughtfman, to delineate an interview, between a Gentleman and Lady enamour'd of
each other, mounted on horfes, labouring
under the infirmity mentioned in the above
letter.   The attitude of the animals, at thefe
times, is admirably fingular; and has fuch an
effect on the Rider, as always to attract his
eyes towards the tail, to fee what is the
matter.   Indeed the back becomes fomewhat
like

like that of a camel, until all is ventilated.
I have feen fo many things of this kind,
that I am concern'd for the young Lady's feelings, on this occafion, knowing they muft be
great. But ftill, thofe feelings, well delineated,
might have as fine an effect as Le Brun's
Paffions.—I fear, however, my friend Wood,
and his prefcriptions, will be in difgrace; for
a day or two ago, the learned Dr. ———
of St. John's College (the fame to which
Mr. Gillyflower belongs), call'd on me for
an ointment, to make the hair grow on his
horfe's tail; and talking about Mr. Gillyflower's horfe, he faid he knew him; that
he had bought him out of the Duke of Nor-
folk's Stud. I then told the Doctor of the
awkward infirmity he had; upon which,
he faid, he was not a bit furpriz'd, for the
horfe was got by Phlegon, and Phlegon was
one of the Sun's horfes he drove in his cha-
riot; and that Phlegon and the other three
were all got by the winds *; fo that no

Wood

---

* Naturum (obferved the Doctor) expellas furca tamen ufque
recurret.

Wood in the kingdom would be able to get his windy tricks out of him.

Mr. Gillyflower being a fcholar, might have known as much, methinks.

G. G.

LETTER THE EIGHTH.

To the Editor of the Annals of Horsemanship.

Mr. GAMBADO,

I AM a tradefman, in the middling way, and keeps a fhop in Holborn, where you may be furnifhed with the beft hofe, of all forts, at the loweft prices; but being determined to pay every one their own, without fwindling, cannot afford to keep a one horfe fhay, or a gigg; and yet having a wife and daughter grown up to woman's eftate, I could wifh, for quietnefs fake, to give them an airing to Highgate, Hampftead, or Hornfey, on a Sunday, like the reft of my neighbours; but this I cannot cleverly do on a fingle horfe,

G   which

which is all I keeps. I was therefore think-
ing, that as you knows all about thefe here
things you might tell me of fome kind of faddle,
whereby it might be done, for we are all of
us little, and very flight. I therefore takes the
liberty of axing your advice, and am ready
to make you the compliment of a pair of beft
boot ftockings for it.

I think it is a fhame the Society of Arts do
not advertife a premium for finding out fome
œconomical fcheme of this nature. Inftead
of which, at this very time, you have a
parcel of fellows who go about teaching folks
to ride on three horfes at once, when as how
there are very few, in a moderate line, that
can afford to keep half a one.

I am, yours, &c.

TIMOTHY LEG.

P. S. I have fome notion the Legs are re-
lated to the Gambadoes. I know we are a-kin
to the boots.

The

The ANSWER.

Mr. LEG.

IF you can purchafe a very long-back'd horfe, the thing you require is very practi-cable, and by one common, and two fide faddles, you may all ride in file, or one be-hind the other ; one lady facing to her right, the other to her left. But if your horfe is of the fhort punchy kind, you may manage the matter nearly in rank, or all in a row, by means of two appendages like pan-niers.

Thus, I think, I can accommodate any body, who has more than two to be convey'd,

and

and is either poſſeſt of a long, or a ſhort-back'd horſe.

I make no doubt but you are connected ſome way or other with us, I therefore have ſent you all the wholeſome advice I could. And as there is no contenting all, I hope, at leaſt, the Legs will be ſatisfied, whoever elſe may grumble.

I am your Friend and Kinſman,

G. GAMBADO.

Your boot ſtockings will be very acceptable, as I have a touch of the gout in my knees.

LETTER

H. Bunbury Esq. Del.̊   W.P. Carey Sculp.

O Me & my Wife and Daughter.
O TERQUE QUATERQUE BEATI.

Publish'd by Wᵐ Jones Dame Street Nᵒ ...

LETTER THE NINTH.

To G. Gambado, *Efq.*

Mr. Gambado,

THE following very fingular affair hap-
pening in my prefence yefterday, I take the
earlieft opportunity of informing you of it:
in hopes, if any other accounts of it fhould
reach you, my ftory may be heard firft.
I was juft come out of my parifh church,
where I had, indiffolubly I fuppofe, united
one John Mudd, to one Elizabeth Middle-
ditch. I was detain'd fome time in the bel-
fry, reprimanding my Clerk for fuffering a
tribe of filthy dogs to be parading the aifle
during the nuptial ceremony; when, on my
                                    entering

entering the church-yard, I defcried John, rather too fweet upon Elizabeth, and con- ducting her among the tomb-ftones, under the large apple-trees. I inftantly fallied to rout them, which, as I was effecting, I heard a noife of a tremendous kind, and looking up, faw (it's a fact) a fierce-look- ing man, mounted on a horfe of great mag- nitude, prancing in the middle of an apple- tree. He fhowered down the pippins like hail upon us, and, as I faw he was about to defcend, I for fear of the worft, took to my heels, and was home, I believe, in a fhorter time by fome minutes than I was the Sun- day before, when there was a danger of a turbot's being overdreft. The parifh have taken it up; and, I underftand, ftories of the turbot are handed about, to hurt me with the Bifhop; and this laft bufinefs of the apple-tree, is turn'd into very fhameful fcandal. But the above is truth, I am reaưy to affirm. I have fince heard, that the figure and horfe came to the earth, and flying over the church-yard wall, were feen no more. I have put fome of the pippins in brandy

(not

(not for eating), as no doubt they will fetch a high price when this ſtory is publicly known. I am told alſo, that after my tak-ing to flight, John and his Mate return'd under the apple-tree, no more diſmay'd than if they had ſeen a common man a horſe-back.

I am, Sir, moſt aſſuredly yours,

G. TACKEM.

Whether this was ſomewhat preternatural or no, I cannot determine. I am a good deal ſtagger'd in my belief, and dare not, at preſent, make public my opinions. But I ſhould be glad to hear yours. I have, however, determin'd to have the apple-trees down.

MY OBSERVATIONS.

THIS is very hard upon the apple-trees, and harder upon thoſe that make pies from them.

The

The ſtory certainly ſeem'd ſurprizing at firſt; and being, I confeſs, a little ſuperſtitious, I ſuſpected my Divine was none of the over-righteous, and that either a ſpirit, or his conſcience, frighted him. But the matter was ſoon clear'd up, by the receipt of the following letter, which came to my hands about five days after the other.

Mr. Sir,

I forgot your name, and ſo got a friend to direct this to you. I am told you are a uſeful man, that you publiſh all you receive, and believe all you publiſh. Now, if you can ſwallow this, you will any thing; though I'll be d——d if it is not true. Laſt Thurſday our hounds ſtarted a hare ſo ſuddenly, whilſt we were chatting and lolling careleſsly, that, by G——, my horſe, who pulls like the devil, was off with me in a jiffey. As ill luck would have it, the curb broke, and he ran ſtraight on for the cliffs above the Scar. I was in a hell of a ſtew, but ſtuck faſt,

and

and pull'd, and haul'd, to try to turn him, but to no purpofe ; for he made a fort of a fhy towards the cliff, and down we both went, by G—d. As good luck would have it, we came plump into a large apple-tree, in a church-yard, where we fwung for fome time, but the boughs gave way, and brought us fafe and found to land. I tipp'd my nag over a broken place in the wall, and foon found the hounds again. But the fineft thing of all was, when we firft lit in the apple-tree, up bounced a fine girl from under-neath ; and a moment after, ecod! old Pud-ding-fleeves himfelf, in full regimentals ;   I gave him a tantara, and the Doɛtor ran like a hare. You may infert this if you pleafe, and as it's a faɛt, you may tack my name to it ; being,

Your humble fervant,

HENRY BEAGLE, Jun.

Huntfcrag, Northumberland.

H

OBSER-

OBSERVATIONS.

The above extraordinary affair appeared firſt in the public paper at Newcaſtle, and was afterwards copied into thoſe in London; the anecdote of the Clergyman excepted. I own I did not give credit to it, until I received the above letters, which put it beyond all doubt. For one of my correſpondents was the perſon himſelf who made the extraordinary deſcent; and the Doctor, who vouches for it, I ſhould imagine, had as lieve it had never happened.

It is indeed worthy a place in theſe Annals, as a very ſingular accident; but I know not what knowledge is to be derived from it, except, that a down leap is not ſo very dangerous, provided you have an apple-tree to leap into: at the ſame time, ſuch a tree affords but bad ſhelter for an amour, at leaſt at the foot of a ſteep cliff, as the Doctor muſt admit.

G. G.

LETTER

LETTER THE TENTH.

SIR,

PERMIT me, through the channel of the Penny Poſt, to addreſs you on a ſubject I do not entirely underſtand; and which you, no doubt, from the eminence of your name, are a moſt complete maſter of. I have bought a grey gelding lately, which I never had ſeen out of the ſtable, but he look'd a very grand figure in a ſtall, and they aſſured me he was found: ſo, Sir, I bought him, and the next day mounted and rode him to Chiſwick. The horſe, Sir, I preſumed went oddly; and I got the hoſtler of the King of Bohemia to get up inſtead of me, and let me ſee him go. He went ex-

H 2   tremely

tremely well with his fore legs, juſt clearing
the ground; but he lifted up his hind ones
as if he was dancing, or drunk: it is the
moſt fantaſtic way of going I ever ſaw; and
I ſent, and ſaid I ſhould return him: the
gentleman ſaid no—that a horſe could not
go too much above his ground; and if it
was with his hind legs, it was better he
ſhould do ſo, than trip before and behind
too.

I wiſh to know your opinion upon this:
whether I muſt take him, or not.   I am
the joke of the road wherever I go, and the
blackguards adviſe me to ride him tail fore-
moſt.   I don't love a joke eſpecially wherein
concern'd myſelf; and rather than have another cut upon me, I ſhall cut riding entirely, and ſell this palfrey of mine to the pro-
prietors of the Brentford Fly.   It is a pity,
Sir, that there is not room in the Leverian, or any other Muſeum, to exhibit the
extraordinary motions of Bipeds and Qua-
drupeds; which, I think, are often more
wonderful than their ſtructure.   Had there
been

been fuch a convenience, I could have fold my horfe for a hundred guineas, as a fhew; and provided for a damn'd old Uncle of mine, that is always in my way. Awaiting your anfwer,

   I am, Sir,

     Your moft refpectful Servant,

       R. MORECRAFT, Jun.

Seething Lane, London.

N. B. Having juft mentioned what I could fell my horfe for, under particular circum-ftances; I muft beg you, at the fame time, to underftand, that he is at your fervice for five guineas.

 G. Gambado, Efq.

Memorandum to Letter the Tenth.

I remember anfwering this flippant young gentleman. But I could neither make him

        com-

comprehend, that his horfe was afflicted with a double portion of the String Halt, or that he was to give me a fee for my trouble. So our correfpondence clofed. But the horfe is actually to be feen going, four times a day, in the Greenwich, not the Brentford, Fly, with a dog on his back; and fo very rare and uncouth is his method of handling his hind legs, that I have never feen fo extraordinary an inftance of excellence in canine equitation.

G. G.

N. B. The Public to be told, I am not to be trifled with. This young gentleman never wanted my advice, I dare fay; put me to fome expence in letters, about a damn'd horfe, which he had better have given to his Uncle at once, for his own riding. I don't love a joke myfelf.

LETTER

LETTER THE ELEVENTH.

To Mr. GEOFFREY GAMBADO.

SIR,

THE following Extract of a Letter from Newmarket fell into my hands lately, near Chester. It contains an account of so extraordinary and severe a race, and exhibits such an instance of bottom in three horses, as can scarcely be parallel'd in the annals of racing. I hope it comes under the description that will gain it admittance into your publication. I have made much enquiry at Newmarket about it, and can only make out, that the Oldest Jockies suppose it to be a letter

from

from the Duke of Wharton to Sir William More, in Chefhire, who was his confederate on the turf.

I am, Sir,

Your very humble Servant,

JOHN HARMAN.

LETTER

LETTER THE TWELFTH.

Extract of a Letter from Newmarket.

THURSDAY.

" THIS Day the following horſes ſtarted
for the King's Plate : Lord Godolphin's b.
H. Shakeſpear, by his Arabian, out of a
True Blue Mare; Lord Portmore's b. H.
Looby, by Bright's Arabian, out of a Partner
Mare ; Mr. Panton's cheſ. H. Partner, by
the Lonſdale Arabian, out of a ſiſter to
Bonny Black. The betts were 2 to 1, the field
againſt Shakeſpear.

1ſt. Heat. Shakeſpear took the lead, and
ſupported it at his uſual deep rate, through
the furzes, to the top of Choakjade, with
Looby in his quarters all the way ; but in

I   coming

coming down the hill, he ran up to him, and they difputed the lead every inch, to the three mile poft, where Looby gain'd about half a length, and kept it, till they came over-againft the Well Gap; but before they reach'd the diftance poft, it was impoffible to difcern which was firft, and they ran in fo clofe together, that it could not be decided which won. Partner laid by, pull'd up, and walk'd in.

2d. Heat. Partner made all the play for the firft two miles; and Looby, perceiving that Shakefpear did not intend to call upon him, begun to be very bufy along the ditch, and gave him fo much trouble upon the flat, that juft as they enter'd the cords, they were both at laps, and ran it every yard in; but Looby being diftreft by the feverity of this, and the firft heat, was forc'd to fubmit to his adverfary, though with great honor, by half a neck. This rais'd the odds to 3 to 1 Shakefpear did not win; which were accepted by the judicious part of the turf, who relied on the Godolphin blood, and the honefty

honefty of the True Blues. Shakefpear went
away brifkly the third Heat, clofely purfu'd
by Partner, while Looby lay too far behind,
to profefs difputing this heat, as he had
bravely done the two firft. They were now
in the third mile, and Partner had never attempted to take the lead; for, as he was
confcious he had the foot, though not the
ftoutnefs of Shakefpear, he intended to re-
ferve his pufh as long as poffible; but
Shakefpear being aware of that, and trufting
to his bottom, began to make running as he
croft the ruts, and difplay'd all his power
upon the flat, with good refolution : but
could not conquer his adverfary, till the
rifing ground from the diftance to the
winning poft, by means of his fuperior
ftrength, declar'd the conteft in his favour,
by half a length, hard run. This brought
the betts to even money, Shakefpear againft
the field.

The 4th Heat they all jump'd off at fcore,
and ran the firft two miles as if they intended to tear one another to pieces; they

I 2   then

then flackened their pace, and came gently together to the flat, when they ran at the top of their fpeed above half a mile, in which they prevail'd by turns; whilft new wagers echoed from the Betting Gap and cords every moment. And now Shakefpear having indulg'd a little pull, in order to have fomething in hand at coming in, was thrown two lengths behind, and the other two continued clofe together, ftuck and cut every yard, when he made a loofe, as his laft effort, and catch'd them within twenty yards of the ending poft, dead run, and their riders almoft exhaufted; when Partner broke down, and Looby yielded the victory, fcarcely by half the head, and with it his life, for he died immediately after the heat.

" The weather is extremely fine, abundance of good company, and the battle was fo equal, that the vanquifh'd difdain'd to mourn, and the victor refus'd to triumph.

Entered

Entered for the Mare's Plate to-morrow.

Juliet, full fifter to Shakefpear.

Cordelia, by Cyprus, out of Bonny Black.

Violante, by Bay Bolton, out of a Snake Mare.

Camilla, by the Curwen b. Barb. out of Roxana's dam.

Rofalinde, by Childers, out of Brockels by Betty.

And my chef. Mare, Arethufa.

" The chief betts at prefent are; even money my mare and Juliet againft the field. They are all in fine condition, and it will undoubtedly be a fmoking heat, for I fhall order my mare to go off at fcore, and run it every yard; you know fhe'll come through without a pull. As foon as the battle is over, I'll fend you an account of the victory by Tom, and am extremely forry that your indifpofition detains you from your favourite diverfion, the turf.

" Hannibal

" Hannibal is fallen lame, and your horfe will win hollow on Saturday. Victim has paid forfeit to my young horfe, and I have match'd him with Pluto for a thoufand."

OBSERVATION.

This was a race indeed, and worthy recording in my Annals. Many thanks to the Correfpondent who communicated it.

G. G.

LETTER

LETTER THE THIRTEENTH.

To G. Gambado, *Efq.*

GOOD SIR,

I A M in great hafte, having a great quick-
nefs of pulfe, and my bed being now warm-
ing; but cannot get into it without informing you how faft I came home from Market
to-night, and upon my old Mare too, who
was always unkind before as to going. But
fo it happened. The old Mare, that I could
never get to go above three miles an hour,
as foon as ever I was up, fet off, and the
                                    devil

devil could not ftop her till fhe got home
—ten miles in about 58 minutes. I'm in a
fweat yet. But I have found out her mo-
tive, and now the Public may make ufe of
it—I had bought a couple of lobfters to carry home, had their claws tied up, and put
one in each of my great coat pockets—Well,
the old gentleman in my right pocket (a cun-
ning one, I warrant him) fomehow or another contrived to difengage his hands, and no
doubt foon applied them to the old Mare's fide,
and, I imagine, had got faft hold of a rib by
the time I reach'd the 1ft mile-ftone; for
fhe was mad I thought, and my hat and
wig were gone in a twinkle—(a wig made by
the man who advertifes they never fly off the
ears—a rafcal—wigs may now be univerfally
complained of). However, when I got off,
and had taken a little breath, I went into
the kitchen to unload, but mift one of my
lobfters; fo I run back into the ftable, and
there was the hero hanging at the old Mare's
fide: fhe'd had enough of it, and fo ftood
quiet. I eat the foldier to-day, and had like

to

How to make the Mare to go.

NON CUT SED QUOMODO

to have died of laughing the whole time.
Now, don't you think a lobfter might turn
to account where a horfe is a little dull or fo
—mind me—if one of thefe fellows is not
worth more than a doz ͼ pair of Mr. Moore's
beft fpurs—I'm a Dͼ ͼhman—for I have
wore out a dozen upon the aforefaid mare
in the courfe of the . fifteen laft years.   It's
eafily done, only putting no handcuffs on
them, and they'll foon go to work and do
your bufinefs.   Pray, Sir, don't you think
they might be of ufe to the light dra-
goons ?

I thought myfelf bound to inform you
of this, as hoping it would prove a great
national difcovery : I mean to keep lobfters
on purpofe, for it's cheaper than buying a
horfe inftead of my old mare ; and I can
go fafter with one of them in my pocket
than I could poft.   When my boys come
home from fchool, to hunt in the foreft, I
mean to treat each of them with a crawfifh for

K   his

his poney, and then, I think, we fhall head
the field.

I am, Sir,

Yours, ever in hafte,

PETER PUFFIN.

LETTER

.

LETTER THE FOURTEENTH.

MR. GAMBADO,

I HAVE juſt received the encloſed letter. As it ſeems worthy publication, I beg you would inſert it in the Annals of Horſeman-ſhip, which I hear you are going to bring out.

I am your humble Servant,

R. TATTERSHALL,

K 2   SIR,

SIR,

AS I cannot conveniently attend in perfon at your celebrated Repofitory at London, and being in great want of fuch a kind of horfe, as I fhall fpecify below, and as I prefume in your own Stud you have more than one, fuch once victorious Steed on the Turf, though fuperannuated for the Race, yet capable of eafy Road exercife (and the Writer here pretends to be as good an Horfe-mafter as any in the Univerfe), I confide on your fuppos'd candour to excufe this liberty, after much debating in my mind, to write immediately to yourfelf (having heard laft fummer Mr. Score, a Flint-merchant, fpeak much to your praife, who dines, he faid, often at your Ordinary). I hope, therefore, you will indulge a Stranger's requeft, as moft probably you may have fuch a Steed (in your own Stud) to difpofe of; which will be efteemed a fingular favour to your unknown, at prefent, though

Very humble Servant,

SAMUEL LANGLEY, (D.D.)

Wanted

Wanted an Horfe, M. or G. of fize and
ftrength, that has figured on the Turf, that
will be fold cheap, as being in years, but
not paft gentle road ufe, perfectly quiet and
temperate, whofe paces are fmooth and eafy
to the Rider, and free from all vice.

P. S. If an Horfe be recommended, I had
rather he had covered, if he will be ridden
on the road in company with a Mare, and
be quiet as a Gelding. But I fhall not approve of one, either blind, lame, or broken-
winded. Stiffnefs at ftarting I fhall not re-
gard it, nor his Age, though in his Teens,
if his conftitution be good, and he can feed
well, and yet go well, and fafely to the Rider.

A line (and I pray fuch compliment may
be fpeedily vouchfafed me) of the Size, Age,
Pedigree, Colour, and his Performances, with
his loweft Price, will be immediately attended to. If I approve of the account, and
the terms, I fhall fend to buy and ride him
down.

down. The diſtance is about 142 miles (mea-
ſured), which he may perform, in 3 or 4 days,
as you ſhall adviſe.

The Rev. Dr. Langley,
Checkley, near Cheadle, Staffordſhire.

CHECKLEY, May, 14, 1789.

LETTER

LETTER THE FIFTEENTH.

To Mr. Gambado.

SIR,

I HAVE long lamented that Riding ſhould be attended with ſuch expence; and ſee no reaſon why many articles attending it, which coſt money, might not as well be diſpenſed with as not. If a Gentleman, when his Bills are brought in, is ſomewhat put to it, to pay for Hay and Corn (which, by the bye, are neceſſary, or his Horſes would be no better than Jack-Aſſes), why ſhould he be ſo very extravagant in the article of Leather? Your Gentleman now-a-days, muſt

have

have to his bridle, two head ftalls, and
two reins; to his faddle, two flaps on each
fide, two girths, a crupper or a breaft plate
—perhaps both, not forgetting a martingale,
with its appendages. I have actually feen a
young Cockader, about town, with a breaft
plate on his horfe, that threw his faddle
forwards, merely to be tafty; whilft his
Companion's nag, who flipt his girths, had
a crupper on like a Dragoon's.   But, Sir,
thefe Chaps are not confined to their expen-
diture in leather—Only obferve the buckles
and ftuds, &c. that ornament their trappings
—Not a bridle, but would furnifh a dozen
of knives and forks—nor a faddle that has
not a tea-kettle and lamp upon it.

Our Forefathers never rode in this way,
and I am happy that I forefee a Revolution is
at hand.

It is needlefs to reprobate fuch expence, as
the Saddler's bill probably brings in the punifh-
ment along with it.

Whether

How to prevent a Horse slipping his Girths.

NON SIBI, SED PATRIA.

Whether Adam, or Cain, or Abel ever rode, it does not appear; but they had Horfes, and Dogs, and Foxes, and Hares; and why are we not to fuppofe that they went a hunting, and had as good fport as we have (nay, better: for they had no Huntfmen)? They muft, however, have rode without faddles, it is pretty clear.

I do not find that thefe fuperfluities were held in much efteem in the time of the Romans. Raphael, in his picture of Attila, at Rome, has treated us with a Hun or two, riding after the fafhion of their country, I fuppofe. The devil a bit of a bridle have they—nothing but a ftrap round their Horfes neck, which they hold at each end with their hands. Nor are their Nags of the quieteft either, but feem to be fhowing their agility and caprioles to the beft advantage. By no means fuch Palfreys as either I, or you Mr. Gambado, would like to beftride without a bridle, and a good plain faddle too.

L   One

One Stanurtius (a very learned old Author), tells us, that in his time, the Wild
Irifh (I don't underftand how he diftin-
guifhes the Wild Irifh) ufed to ride in a
ftrange way, but you muft admit they had no '
bridles.

" Tubaram fetas, aut equorum auriculas
feniftrâ apprehendant; atque dum equi obfti-
pis capitibus quieti fe inclinant, equites,
etiam loricis aut fagis amicti, mera corporis
agilitate fe efferunt, divaricatriq! cruribus
ephippia occupant."

Which may be thus turn'd into Englifh—

" They feize their Horfes manes, or their
ears, with their left hand, and whilft their
Horfes were thus kept fteady, the Riders,
even if covered with their cuiraffes or fa-
gums, exerting a wonderful agility of body,
fpring aftride into the faddle."

By

How to ride without a Bridle?

ORANDUM EST UT SIT MENS SANA IN CORPORE SANO.

By this it appears to be very lucky, that cropping Horfes, was not then the fafhion, or they would have had but little command of them. The Wild Irifh now, I am told have reverfed the mode, and taken up the tail inftead of the poor ears, which are ne-glected.

The Tartars of this day, Mr. Gambado, have no faddles, but ride upon a Beef Steak, or a flice of Horfe-flefh : which, by that means, becomes fufficiently done for them to eat, by the time they have finifh'd their airing. What a delicious fuccedaneum for a faddle ; it anfwers two purpofes at once. If a faddle ever anfwers a fecond, it is, of gall-ing you confoundedly.

I have dropt a hint of a Revolution—and I expect one. Let the Huns look to it ; a fuccefsful experiment of riding in their way, has lately been made in my country ; but whether from motives of œconomy, cu-riofity, or emulation, I am yet to learn.

Mr.

Mr. John Mann, a moſt eminent Taylor of Bury St. Edmunds, was one day obſerved to mount his horſe (which ſtood at the door of a Gentleman's houſe in the neighbourhood) when the bitt was out of his mouth, and, in that manner, to proceed rapidly towards home. My Informant followed him from cu-rioſity; and, from what he could obſerve, ſaw no alteration in his riding except that he reel'd a little at times, a circumſtance exceedingly natural; and although he had three turns to make to the right, and two to the left, to thread the needle through ſome Mackerel carts on the road, and a Wa-ter to paſs; (where, by the bye, he let his horſe ſtop too long, and drink too much), yet he arrived ſafe and ſound at home.

Now conſidering the five angles, the Mac-kerel carts, and his not going over the bridge, which was the right way; I queſtion but ſuch a performance might have puzzled one of At-tila's fellows.

As

As bridles begin to fhake, fo I may well fay, faddles totter. The Tartars muft not think themfelves the only Moderns who ride without them. It was but two years fince, at Afcot Heath, that the thing was attempted and atchiev'd over the Courfe there. Two Gentlemen rode a match, and, wonderful as it appear'd to modern Britons, one was feen to arrive at the ending Poft without his bridle, and the other without his faddle. The latter Gentleman had not even a Beef Steak to fit upon, nothing but a pair of corderoys between him and the Horfe's back, the faddle following him behind like a pillion.

By thefe proficiencies then let us hope, Sir, we may knock off foon a very ufelefs portion of expence—overtake a Hun, and perhaps catch a Tartar.

I am, Sir,

Your obedient Servant,

JOHN HICKATHRIFT.

MY

MY OBSERVATIONS.

The extraordinary performances of the Wild Irifh aftonifh nobody. I never heard of a Hun, when I read Mr. H.'s Letter firft, and thought he meant a Hum. This may be a pretty way of riding, for any thing I know; but I am for a bridle and faddle; and fhall not grudge twenty pennyworth of leather to make a martingale of, if it may fave fome of my teeth. Vale JOHN HICKATHRIFT.

G. G.

LETTER

LETTER THE SIXTEENTH.

GEOFFREY GAMBADO,

EDITOR OF VARIOUS LEARNED PERFORMANCES.

SIR,

YOU have, no doubt, heard of the defcription of Natural Philofophers, called
Pigeon Fanciers, who breed the bird of
that name, and all its varieties. I was
once, Sir, a member of this community, till
growing tir'd of Pouters, Tumblers, Nuns,
Croppers, Runts, &c. &c. I was refolved
to enlarge my ideas, by extending my re-
fearches, and abandoning the Biped, to obtain a clofer acquaintance with the Qua-
druped, I became a Horfe Fancier. Being
fond of riding, and daily obferving, in my
airings to Brentford, a very great variety of

horfes,

horſes, and a ſtill greater variety in their
motions ; I ſome years ſince ſet about mak-
ing a collection of ſuch as were ſingular, and
eccentric in their ſhapes and actions, and
flatter myſelf no private muſeum can have boaſt-
ed of a more admirable variety, than I have
poſſeſſed.   I mean ſome day or other to claſs
them, and by ſo doing, think I ſhall be able to
convince the Naturaliſts, that from their form
and performances, many horſes are allied to
the cow, and ſome to the hog kind.   In the
mean time, I ſhall juſt mention to you a few
varieties of this ſame animal, which I have had
in my poſſeſſion ; and which may, perhaps,
afford you an hour or two's amuſement and reflection.

I luckily pick'd up a Daiſy-cutter, by his
throwing me down on the ſmootheſt part of the
graſs, in Hyde Park.   I had heard of this de-
ſcription of horſe frequently, but could not believe the accounts of it, till I found it verified,
by experiencing his accompliſhments myſelf.
It ſeems a problem difficult to ſolve, how a
horſe can put forward his fore legs, without
bending

A Daisy Cutter with his Varieties.

INGREDITURQ SOLO & CAPUT INTER NUBILA CONDIT.

bending a joint of them, or, how he can meet
with an impediment to throw him down upon
ground perfectly fmooth !—but fo it is. The
Daify-cutter is admirably eafy in his motion, and having once made the experiment,
upon, and from his back, I am perfectly fa-
tisfied, and now keep him for my wife's own
riding.

Of this variety, there is ftill a variety: this
horfe I likewife poffefs, and keep as a curiofi-
ty. I imagine he muft come from fome dif-
tant country, although he is nick'd after the
Englifh fafhion; for I cannot get any native
to ride him twice.—I have tried a Frenchman
with no better fuccefs. All declining a fecond attempt. This animal refembles the
Daify-cutter perfectly in the ufe of his fore
legs: but, inftead of carrying his head and
neck horizontally, like him, they are raifed
fo high, that his ears are in a perpendicular line
with the pommel of the faddle, and his eyes
always fix'd on the heavens. His fore parts,
when in motion, by this means, much re-
femble a double fifh-hook, or an anchor, as

M   thus

thus ⟨figure⟩ and I therefore propofe to clafs him under one of thefe denomina-
tions.

The Threatener is another of this fpecies
that ought not to be forgot, and indeed he
feldom is by any one who has once poffefs'd
him.   By the Threatener, Man himfelf, the
Lord of the Creation, who fubdues all the
animals that range the foreft, is himfelf kept
in fear and trepidation.   This ingenious animal has the fagacity at every ftep to threa-
ten the fracture of his rider's neck; probably with a view to difcourage and even
abolifh the cuftom of riding in general:
and at the fame time the good fenfe not to
fall quite down, left, he fhould accidentally
break his own.   As amongft pigeons, fo
amongft horfes, there are Tumblers. The feat
is, however, performed differently, and varies
confiderably in its effects on the performers.
As the pigeon executes this without any thing

on

The Tumbler or its Affinities.

CAVAT LAPIDEM NON VI, SED SÆPE CADENDO.

Dublin Published by W. Jones N°86, Dame Street.

A Horse with a Nose

HOC SIGNO VINCES

on its back; fo the horfe feldom atchieves it, without fomebody upon his. To the latter therefore we muft give the greateft fhare of merit, who ventures to perform upon a hard road what the other does only in the air, without even a cloud to brufh againft. The one preferring, it feems, the Milky, and the other the Highway.

Amongft horfes I have never difcovered a Pouter; but I have had a fine Puffer *. The noife he made, however, and particularly when at his bufinefs, was not pleafant; and I let a neighbour have him cheap, who had a good three-ftall mufeum, and a very heavy vehicle to draw; fo that in all weathers he might enjoy the entertainment of his very extraordinary qualifications.

It is well known that there is a horfe that is a Carrier, fo is there a pigeon like-
M 2 wife.

---

* The Puffer, if properly kept on plenty of hay and water, and with little exercife, will in a fhort time gratify his Keeper by changing into another variety, which we call a Roarer.

wife. But as it may not be known to every one, I muft inform you, Sir, that, from very long obfervation, I find the pigeon is the moft expeditious of the two.

·I am at this moment, Sir, in poffeffion of a horfe that has a Nofe, if I may fo call the fenfe of fmelling in a high degree: I do not perceive that he often hits upon game as the dog does, but he makes for a ftable door with great avidity; nay, fo certain is he of difcovering where victuals and drink are to be had, that it is with the utmoft difficulty I can get him to pafs a fign-poft; and it requires no fmall exertion of arms and legs to prevent his running into every alehoufe on the road with me. Thefe are evident figns of a very fine nofe: it is a little inconvenient, to be fure, particularly if one is in hafte; but the qualification is fingular. This variety I call the Setter, both from his poffeffing the faculties of the dog fo called, and from his pronenefs to fet down his load wherever entertainment for man and horfe are to be found. I fhall not at prefent

enter

enter into more varieties, but poftpone my
communications to another opportunity : only
having juft touch'd upon the horfe with a Nofe,
I muft inform you, that one of my neighbours,
an Attorney, tells me he has a horfe, that has
no mouth.   Although my ftalls are all full, I
fhall certainly purchafe this uncommon animal,
if he is to be had ; as, from his formation,
the poffeffion of him can be attended with
little or no expence but the prime coft.

    I am Sir,

     Your very humble Servant,

           BENJ. BUFFON.

              LETTER

LETTER THE SEVENTEENTH.

To Mr. GAMBADO.

SIR,

INTENDING the following account of a moſt extraordinary phænomenon that appeared in our pariſh two days ſince, for the Philoſophical Tranſactions; I ſhould not have ſent it to you, but that there was a horſe concern'd in it, and ſo ſtrange a one, that I thought that if you were not inform'd of it, you would be concern'd yourſelf. I have drawn it up to the beſt of my abilities. It is as follows:

On

On the morning of the 6th inftant, the weather intenfely cold, the ground covered with ice or frozen fnow, as I may fay, pre-cifely at the hour of eight, A. M. as Mary Jenkins (who lives as fervant at the Fox and Crown public-houfe, juft on the brow of Highgate Hill), a young woman about nine-teen years of age, of a frefh complexion and fanguine habit, was lying awake in her bed (Reaumur's Thermometer then ftanding at only   and Fahrenheit's at   ), fhe heard a fhout of an uncommon kind; and running to the window, the following phæ-nomenon prefented itfelf to her view. A man, dreft much after the manner of the Englifh, but of a fierce and terrifying afpect, feem'd to pafs the Fox like lightning, mount-ed on fomething like a horfe; but fuch a one as fhe had never before feen; having the head, neck, and fore-legs of thofe of this country; faving that the legs were ftretch'd out and void of motion; he was furnifh'd with a pair of wings, and his hind parts de-fcended from his head obliquely to the ground.

She

She verily believes he had a forked tail, but that hind-legs he had none. The man fat very ftiff and upright, and continued his fhouts (which from what I can make out from the Girl's imitations of them much refembled the war-hoops of the Indians), until he turned the corner by the Boarding-fchool, where fhe loft fight of him. But he was again vifible to her naked eye at the foot of the hill; when fome fleet falling, he wholly difappeared.

The poor Girl, exceedingly terrified, awakened the family, and was ordered to go to Dr. ———, to take oath of what fhe had feen; which fhe did.

Being one of the firft who heard of it, I buftled about, and got a good deal of information concerning the progrefs of the phænomenon, and think I can afcertain at about what rate he travelled.

As the clock ftruck eight, Mary Jenkins faw him on the brow of the hill.

Mamfelle

Mamſelle Bellefeſſe, the Teacher at the
Boarding-ſchool, being call'd up before her
time, and in a ſmall building which looks
into the road juſt at the turn, her watch
luckily by her ſide, ſaw the ſtrange gentleman paſs, preciſely at eight and three ſeconds.
She deſcribes him differently from Mary Jenkins, though they both agree in the wings.
" Il me ſembloit avoir le viſage de Cupidon
" avec les ailes de Pſyche *"—ſays Mamſelle de B.   At eight and ſix ſeconds the
Blind Beggar, by his computation, heard
him paſs the Cheeſe-cake Houſe.   At eight
and eight ſeconds A. M. the man coming to
ſweep the chimneys met him at the finger-
poſt.   In a ſecond after, he knock'd down and
went over Alice Turner, the Saloup Woman ; and exactly at eight and ten ſeconds,
Mary Jenkins ſaw the laſt of him.   Now
calculating the ſeconds and the diſtances
between each ſpot where he was ſeen, it
is evident he went at a prodigious rate.

N   Childers

---

* Which I learn means —He ſeem'd to have the face of Cupid
and Pſyche's wings.

Childers would have been a fool to him·
But he had wings, indeed, which perhaps
may be more ufeful than hind-legs, otherwife I
could not have conceived it.

That there are horfes of this kind in nature I make no doubt; as the Lords of the
Admiralty authorife us to believe it, by ex-
hibiting two in the front of their Houfe of
Office at Whitehall. To thefe horfes Mary
Jenkins's feems to be nearly allied; and perhaps by enquiring at the Admiralty we may
be inform'd where they may be had. As we
lye on the great North Road, I fhould fuppofe this, that came through our town, might
be what they call a fea-horfe, and come from
Lapland or thereaways.

If you can throw any light on this wonderful
phænomenon, Sir, I hope you will make it public for the good of the community.

I am, Sir,

Your humble Servant,

WILLIAM GORGET,

Surgeon.

Highgate, Feb. 26th.

P. S.

P. S. I can't get it out of my head the pace the Gentleman went, confidering the interruption he met with from riding over the Saloup Woman.

The Parifh Officers had a long meeting about this ftrange man that fhew'd his face here. But I foon convinced 'em he had not ftaid long enough in the parifh to gain a fettlement; and fo they are eafy. But there's great debates in the Veftry, and in the Coffee-houfe, and Mr. Figg's fhop yet about it.

MY OBSERVATIONS.

I was much ftaggered when I read this account firft; but finding, on enquiry, that Mr. GORGET, the Surgeon, was a Barber, I grew eafier, and was no more afraid of the North Road than any other—I fhall however

be

be a little more cautious of the folks that lye on it.

After all the inveſtigations that have been made about the Phænomenon of Highgate Hill, and the ſearch into all books that treat of Witchcraft; Glanville, and Moore and Wanley: and after all the controverſy that has been entered into by the unhappy inhabitants, which has thrown that wretched pariſh into more diſtraction than ever fell to the ſhare of St. Paul in Covent Garden! No Vagrants paſt on—No Vagabonds taken up—No Turncocks to be found—all the Water at a ſtop—all the Gin a-going—How ſatisfactory muſt a glimmering of light be to theſe unfortunate Highgates which may open their eyes a little, and reſtore that harmony amongſt them they have been ſo long unacquainted with.

Having received the following Letter a few days ſince, I beg leave to recommend it to the peruſal of the Nobility and Gentry of Highgate

Highgate in general; but more particularly to
Alice Turner (the Saloup Woman, if ſhe is
ſtill extant), to the Chimney Sweeper, the
Blind Beggar (ſomebody muſt read it to him),
Mamſelle Bellefeſſe, and Mary Jenkins; being
convinced, that if the ſtrange perſonage they
ſaw was not Mr. James Jumps, it muſt have
been a Conjurer or Cupid, Pſyche or the
Devil himſelf.

G. G.

LETTER

LETTER THE EIGHTEENTH.

JEFFREY GAMBADO, *Esq*.

KIND SIR,

I HAVE an extraordinary ſtory to tell you, that happened to me t'other day as I was a bringing two pair of ſtays to Miſs Philpot's, at Kentiſh-town. I lives, Sir, at Finchley; and a-top of Highgate Hill my horſe makes a kind of ſlip with his hind feet, do you ſee, for it was for all the world like a bit of ice the whole road. I'd nothing for't but to hold faſt round his neck, and to ſqueeze me elbows in to keep the ſtays ſafe; and, egod, off we ſet, and never ſtopt till I got to the bottom. He never moved a leg didn't my horſe, but ſlided promiſcuouſly, as I may

ſay,

How to travel upon two Legs in a Frost.

OSTENDUNT TERRIS HUNC TANTUM FATA NEQUE ULTRA ESSE FINENT.

fay, till he overfate fomebody on the road;
I was too flurrifome to fee who; and the firft
body I fee'd it was a poor man axing charity
in a hat. My horfe muft have had a rare
bit of bone in his back, and I fit him as
ftiff as buckram.

Your Honour's obedient Servant,

JAMES JUMPS.

F I N I S.

www.ingramcontent.com/pod-product-compliance
Lightning Source LLC
Chambersburg PA
CBHW021134020726
47500CB00003B/1066